AF604486

for ANNA

First published in Australia in 2024 by Thames & Hudson Australia
Wurundjeri Country, 132A Gwynne Street, Cremorne, Victoria 3121

27 26 25 5 4 3

ISBN 978-1-76076-464-7

A catalogue record for this book is available from the National Library of Australia

Typeset in New Century Schoolbook
Printed and bound in China by C&C Offset Printing Co., Ltd

Thames & Hudson Australia wishes to acknowledge that Aboriginal and Torres Strait Islander peoples are the first storytellers of this nation and the Traditional Custodians of the land on which we live and work. We acknowledge their continuing culture and pay respect to Elders past and present.

thamesandhudson.com.au

We Live in a Bus

DAVE PETZOLD

We live in a bus.
She's called Gracie
Joy Rufus Bean
(we couldn't agree
on a name).

Gracie Joy Rufus
Bean has six wheels
and a door that
opens when you
push a button.

Tic-shhh!

Over there is
the kitchen.
This is where I sleep
on the top bunk,
and that's Blob,
the bus spider.

When it's time to go we all help to pack up.

Suzy puts the food scraps in the compost.

Mum rolls up the awning.

Dad cleans
the solar panels

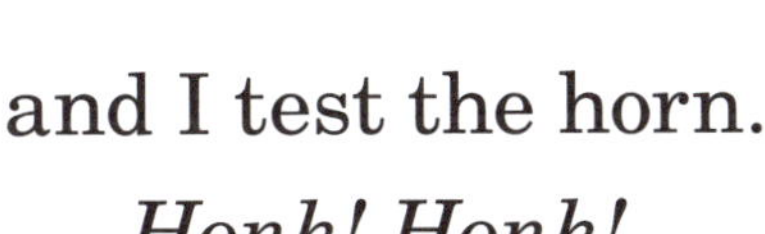

and I test the horn.
Honk! Honk!

Today, it’s my turn to ride up front with Mum.
‘Watch out for the lizards!’ I shout.

Budgies fly from the scrub as we roll by.
Cheep! Cheep! Cheep! Cheep!

We live in a bus
and we stop
wherever we like.

In a small town
we discover a
musical fence.

I play on a rusty,
homemade drum kit.

Dong! Tink! Tong!

In the afternoon
we hike down into
a gorge and swim
in a waterhole.

Dragonflies zip and
zoom high above.

Whizz! Whoosh! Whirr!

We live in a bus and we like to camp in the bush
and sleep under the stars.

When it's cold we make a fire and toast marshmallows.
Crackle! Pop!

On a long, straight road Gracie Joy Rufus Bean gets a flat tyre and we have to pull over to change it.

Pete the truckie helps Dad tighten the bolts.

Tat-tat-tat-tat-tat!

We wait in a sunflower field.
It's hot and stuffy.

Butterflies bounce from flower to flower.
Flitter-flutter! Flitter-flutter!

One morning we visit Ranger Jess who shows us how to listen to Country.

'When you see the red-tailed black cockatoo, rain is coming,' she says.

Aaaaark! Aaaaark!

We look at the small things,

the big things,

and all the things in-between.

We live in a bus and we meet lots of people wherever we go, people who are travelling for a week,

or maybe a year.
Just like us.

Tonight we are sleeping next to a creek.
It's so quiet, except for the frogs.

Pobblebonk! Reeeeeeet!
Tok! Tok!

OPEN
CLOSE

In the morning
the frogs are quiet.

'Where should we go
today?' Dad asks.

'Wherever the road
will take us!'
we all shout.

I push the button.

Tic-shhhh!